Books by Jacqueline Harvey

CLEMENTINE ROSE

and the Surprise Visitor

Jacqueline Harvey

RANDOM HOUSE AUSTRALIA

A Random House book
Published by Random House Australia Pty Ltd
Level 3, 100 Pacific Highway, North Sydney NSW 2060
www.randomhouse.com.au

First published by Random House Australia in 2012

Addresses for companies within the Random House Group can be found
at www.randomhouse.com.au/offices.

National Library of Australia
Cataloguing-in-Publication Entry

Author: Harvey, Jacqueline
Title: Clementine Rose and the surprise visitor
ISBN: 978 1 74275 541 0 (pbk.)
Series: Harvey, Jacqueline. Clementine Rose; 1
Target audience: For primary school age
Dewey number: A823.4

Cover and internal illustrations by J.Yi
Cover design by Leanne Beattie
Internal design by Midland Typesetters
Typeset in ITC Century 12.5/19 by Midland Typesetters, Australia
Printed in Australia by Griffin Press, an accredited ISO AS/NZS
14001:2004 Environmental Management System printer

Random House Australia uses papers that are natural, renewable and
recyclable products and made from wood grown in sustainable forests.
The logging and manufacturing processes are expected to conform to
the environmental regulations of the country of origin.

*For Linsay and Julie, who helped dream
her up, and for Ian, as always*

DINNER ROLLS

Clementine Rose was delivered not in the usual way, at a hospital, but in the back of a mini-van, in a basket of dinner rolls. There was no sign of any mother or father.

Pierre Rousseau, the village baker, had made several stops that morning before his last call at the crumbling mansion known as Penberthy House, on the edge of the village of Penberthy Floss. As Pierre's van skidded to a halt on the gravel drive at the back door, he thought he heard a faint meowing sound.

'Claws, that better not be you back there,' Pierre grouched. He wondered if he had yet again managed to pick up Mrs Mogg's cheeky tabby when he stopped to make his delivery at the general store. Claws had a habit of sneaking on board when Pierre wasn't looking and had often taken the trip around the village with him.

But Claws did not reply.

Pierre hopped out of the van and walked around to the side door. A faded sign in swirly writing said 'Pierre's Patisserie – cakes and pastries of distinction'. He grabbed the handle and slid open the panel.

'Good morning, Pierre,' a voice called from behind him.

'Good morning, Monsieur Digby,' Pierre called back. 'You must 'ave a full 'ouse this weekend, *non*?'

'No, Lady Clarissa just likes to be prepared in case there's a last-minute rush,' said Digby.

But there never *was* a last-minute rush. Digby Pertwhistle had been the butler at Penberthy House for almost fifty years. He had started working for Lord and Lady Appleby as a young man and when they both passed away over twenty years ago their only child, Lady Clarissa, had taken charge. Digby loved Lady Clarissa like a daughter.

As well as the house, Lady Clarissa had inherited a small sum of money from her parents. But Penberthy House had sixty rooms and a roof that leaked in at least sixty places. Soon the money had all been spent and there were still more repairs to be done. So to help pay the bills, Lady Clarissa had opened the house to guests as a country hotel. Unfortunately, business wasn't exactly booming. Penberthy Floss was a very pretty village but it was a little out of the way.

Although Lady Clarissa didn't always have the best of luck with the house, she had the most incredible good fortune with competitions. It had started years ago when she was just

3

a child. With her mother's help she had sent off an entry to the newspaper to win a pony. Three days before her ninth birthday, a letter had arrived to say that she was the winner of a shaggy Shetland, which she called Princess Tiggy. Her love of contests had continued and everyone in the village knew of Lady Clarissa's winning ways. Mrs Mogg would put aside newspapers and magazines and make sure that she marked all of the competitions available.

Over the years, Lady Clarissa had won lots of different things that helped her keep the house running. There were electrical appliances, a kitchen makeover and even several holidays which she gave to Mr Pertwhistle in return for his hard work. She often gave prizes she didn't need to her friends in the village too. They frequently protested and said that she should sell her winnings and pay for the upkeep of the house, but Lady Clarissa would have none of it. If Penberthy House was a little chilly from time to time, or they had to keep a good supply of buckets to set around the place whenever it rained, it didn't matter. Just as long as the people she cared about had everything they needed.

But that's all quite beside the point. This morning there was a delivery that would change Lady Clarissa's life more than any prize could.

Pierre Rousseau and Digby Pertwhistle were standing beside the delivery van chatting about the weather when Pierre put his forefinger to his lips.

'Shhh, did you 'ear that?' he whispered.

'What?' Digby replied. The old man cocked his head and frowned.

'That noise, like a kitten,' Pierre explained.

'No, I don't hear anything but I'd better take those rolls and get a move on,' Digby said as he glanced into the van. They were entertaining three guests that evening. It wasn't exactly a full house, but more visitors than in the past few weekends. Perhaps things were looking up.

Digby pulled the basket towards him. He

picked it up from the edge of the van and staggered under the weight.

'Good grief, man! What did you put in these rolls? Bricks?' Digby exclaimed.

'What do you mean?' asked Pierre, looking shocked.

Digby Pertwhistle handed him the basket and Pierre strained under the unexpected weight. '*Sacrebleu!* My rolls are as light as a feather. That rotten Claws, he must be 'iding in the bottom of this basket. My bread will be ruined.'

Pierre lifted the tea towel that was covering the rolls.

His mouth fell open. He looked, then gently put the basket back down in the van, rubbed his eyes and looked again.

Digby Pertwhistle looked too.

Both men stared at each other and then at the basket. Fresh white dinner rolls surrounded a tiny face with rose-pink lips and bright blue eyes.

Pierre finally found his voice. 'That's not Claws. It's a baby.'

'It's a baby, all right,' Digby agreed. 'But where did it come from? And more importantly, who does it belong to?'

Pierre reached into the basket and gently lifted the infant out. It was dressed in a pink jumpsuit and had a fluffy white blanket around it. Pinned to the blanket was an envelope addressed to Lady Clarissa Appleby, Penberthy House.

'It's not my usual delivery,' Pierre said. 'But it is meant for Lady Clarissa.'

'How did the baby get into the van?' Digby Pertwhistle wondered out loud.

'It must have been when I was at Mrs Mogg's store,' Pierre replied. 'But I don't remember seeing anyone in the village.'

Cradling the tiny child in his arms, Pierre Rousseau, followed closely by Digby Pertwhistle, made the most important delivery of his life.

Lady Clarissa was in the kitchen up to her elbows in washing up. A newborn baby was the last thing she expected on that sunny spring day. But Lady Clarissa took the child's arrival in her stride, just as she did most things.

The note pinned to the baby's blanket read:

Dear Lady Clarissa,

Her name is Clementine Rose and she is yours. The papers attached to this letter say so. No one can take her from you. Please do not look for me. I came on the wind and now I am gone.

Love her, as I wish I could have done.

E

Pierre suggested they call the police. 'It's not right to find a baby in a basket of dinner rolls,' he declared.

Digby added, 'It's not right to find a baby without a mother.'

But from the moment Lady Clarissa locked eyes with Clementine Rose, a bond was struck. Lady Clarissa was in love. Digby Pertwhistle was too. And the paperwork was all in order.

The old man bustled about the house

finding this and that. He remembered that Lady Clarissa's baby things had been stored years ago in the attic and, without a word of prompting, he set off to find what he could.

Pierre disappeared into the village and returned with a box of baby requirements. He bought nappies and formula and even dummies and bibs. He had two young children of his own. His daughter Sophie was just a month old, so he knew a lot about babies.

'Mrs Mogg, she will come and 'elp tonight with your guests,' he explained.

Clementine Rose gurgled and cooed, she slept and she ate. But she hardly ever cried. It was as if she knew right from that first moment how much she was loved and adored, even though she was far too young to understand it at all. And over the years she grew up and no one could remember what life had been like before that fateful morning she arrived in the basket of dinner rolls.

THE LETTER

Clementine Rose stared at her reflection in the hall mirror. She wrinkled her nose and furrowed her brow and concentrated as hard as she could. She stared and stared, her blue eyes gazing back at her like pools of wet ink. But no matter how long she thought about it, her ears simply would not wiggle.

'How do you do that, Uncle Digby?' Clementine turned around and looked at Digby Pertwhistle as his rather large ears flapped like washing.

'Years of practice,' the old man replied.

'But I practise every time I walk past this mirror,' she said, 'and no matter how hard I try, my ears don't wiggle at all.'

Digby looked at her and smiled. 'You're good at lots of other things, Clemmie.'

'Like getting into trouble,' Clementine replied. 'I'm good at that.'

Digby grinned at her. It was true that the child had a knack for getting into all sorts of scrapes, even when she wasn't trying.

'Clementine, are you up there?' her mother called from the bottom of the stairs. 'I'm going to see Mrs Mogg and collect the mail. Would you like to come?'

'Yes, please,' Clementine called back. 'But I'm still in my pyjamas.'

The telephone rang before Lady Clarissa could reply. She walked over to the hall table and picked up the receiver.

'Good morning, Penberthy House, this is Clarissa,' she said. 'Oh, hello Odette, how are you?'

On hearing that name, Clementine ran halfway down the staircase towards her mother.

'Yes, of course we'd love to have Sophie and Jules. That's fine. No, no guests on Sunday night. It's no problem at all. We'll see you then. Bye,' Clarissa said and hung up.

'Are Sophie and Jules coming?' Clementine called. She was bouncing up and down on the spot like Tigger.

'Yes, on Sunday. Pierre and Odette are going to look at a new van and its hours away. They're going to stay in Downsfordvale for the night.'

Clementine's eyes lit up. Sophie was her best friend and Jules was Sophie's brother, who was two years older.

'I can't wait!' Clementine was already thinking about all the things they could do.

'Well, you'd better run along and get dressed quick smart if you want to come with me to the village, Clemmie. We have some guests arriving this afternoon and I need to get back and make a start on dinner,' her mother instructed.

Clementine skittered back upstairs to the landing.

'And I'd better get on and dust those bedrooms,' said Digby. He turned from the mirror he was polishing and grinned at Clementine. 'We don't want our guests complaining about grubby rooms.'

'No, that's true. There are enough other things they can complain about,' she replied. She was thinking of the previous weekend, when a lady called Mrs Pink ran screaming into the hallway saying there was a snake under her bed. Clementine was in her room on the third floor when she heard the commotion and suddenly remembered that she had been playing in that room the day she lost her giant rubber python. It seemed Mrs Pink had found it and wasn't at all happy about it.

Lady Clarissa had to give the woman three cups of tea and a promise of a reduced charge before she'd go back into the room. Clementine was sent to apologise to Mrs Pink, who spent ten minutes telling her off for being so careless with her things, and then the next hour complaining about her sore feet and her bad back and her creaky bones. Clementine had decided right there and then that getting old was not a very sensible thing to do.

Now Clementine ran off to her bedroom. She had been sick with a cold all week and was looking forward to getting out of the house. And she couldn't wait for Sophie and Jules to come on Sunday too.

'There you are, Lavender.' Clementine found her pet lying in the basket on the floor at the end of her bed. 'We're going to see Mrs Mogg.'

Lavender looked up and grunted.

Clementine thought for a moment about what she would wear and then got dressed as quickly as her fingers would allow. She snapped Lavender's lead onto her collar and together the two of them hurried downstairs to meet her mother.

'Oh, Clemmie, that looks lovely. A little overdressed for collecting the mail, perhaps, but I think Mrs Mogg will be thrilled to see you in it,' Lady Clarissa commented.

Clementine twirled around. 'Mrs Mogg makes the best dresses in the whole world.'

Clementine wore a navy smocked tunic and her favourite red patent Mary Jane shoes. Lavender, her tiny teacup pig, wore a sparkling ruby-red collar, which matched Clementine's shoes perfectly.

Lady Clarissa tucked Clementine's blonde hair behind her ear and re-clipped her red bow.

Lavender squealed.

'And I'm sure that Mrs Mogg will notice how lovely you look in your new collar too, Lavender,' said Lady Clarissa as she reached down and patted the top of the tiny silver pig's head.

No one knew where Clementine got her sense of style but it was there, all right. As a baby she would point at things she liked and wave away anything that she didn't want to wear.

Given the poor state of Lady Clarissa's bank balance, she couldn't afford to buy much for

Clemmie. But dear Mrs Mogg loved to sew and as a result Clementine had a huge wardrobe of clothes to wear for every occasion. The child especially adored dresses and as Mrs Mogg loved to make them for her, it was a match made in heaven.

Clementine held Lavender's lead and the three of them took their usual shortcut into the village. They walked through the field at the back of the garden, over the stone bridge across the stream and finally through the churchyard of St Swithun's, where Father Bob was tending his roses by the fence. His ancient bulldog, Adrian, was fast asleep, snoring, on the steps of the church. In the driveway of the rectory next door, Clementine Rose could see Father Bob's shiny new hatchback gleaming proudly in the sun. Her mother had won the little car but decided that Father Bob had much more use for it than she did.

'Good morning, Lady Clarissa. Good morning, Clementine,' he called. 'And good morning, Lavender,' he said in a funny deep voice.

'Hello Father Bob,' the two called back. Lavender squeaked her hello.

'Your roses are looking magnificent,' Clarissa said.

'Thank you, dear. Just between us,' he said, and tapped his finger to his nose, 'I'm hoping for a win at the Highton Mill flower show, God willing. I seem to lose out to Mr Greening from Highton Hall every year and I think it's about time I took home the cup. That one there,' he said, pointing at a particularly beautiful crimson rose, 'is called William Shakespeare and it might just do it for me.'

Clementine skipped over to the fence and pulled one of the blooms towards her.

'Careful, Clemmie,' her mother called, but it was too late. The stem snapped and the perfect rose fell to the ground.

'Oops!' Clementine exclaimed. 'I'm sorry.'

'It's all right, Clementine,' said Father Bob. He walked over and picked it up. 'It's weeks until the show and that flower would have long been finished. Take it with you.' He handed her the stem.

'I didn't mean to break it,' she replied.

Father Bob waved her away. 'Of course you didn't. It's just a rose, Clementine. Another will grow in its place, my dear.'

The child smiled, even though she wasn't entirely sure she was happy. She hoped that Father Bob was telling the truth when he said he didn't mind.

Clarissa and Clementine said goodbye and together with Lavender they walked out through the stone gateway at the front of the church and across the road to the store. Mrs Mogg's old tabby cat, Claws, was sunning himself on the bench seat on the veranda. Clementine reached down to give him a pat and he purred like a diesel engine. Lavender knew better than to come within the cat's reach, having been scratched on the snout several times before. A bell tinkled as Clarissa opened the shop door.

Clementine leaned over and nuzzled her

neck against Claws's face. She was rewarded with a sandpapery lick on her ear.

'Yuck, Claws, that's revolting.' She wiped her ear, then tied Lavender's lead to the opposite end of the bench. She patted the pig's head and followed her mother into the store. Clementine loved its smells: cold ham, hot pies, musk lollies and most of all Mrs Mogg, who smelt like rose petals and powder.

'Good morning,' chirped Margaret Mogg. She was standing behind the counter carefully placing a batch of fresh scones onto a cake stand. 'And don't you look lovely, young lady,' she said to Clementine.

'It's my favourite,' Clementine replied.

'Well, let me have a proper look at you then.' Mrs Mogg twirled her finger and Clemmie spun around. 'Gorgeous. But I've got another on the go.' She winked as she reached under the counter and pulled out some pink polka dot material. 'What do you think about this, then?'

'I love it!' Clementine exclaimed.

'Margaret, you spoil her,' said Clarissa, shaking her head.

'There's nothing else I'd rather be doing. As long as Clementine is happy to wear my clothes, I'm very happy to make them.'

Margaret Mogg turned away from the counter and pulled a pile of mail out of one of the pigeonholes on the wall behind her. Her general store also housed the post office. Everyone in the village had their own little slot in the wall.

She handed Clarissa a small bundle of letters and retrieved a stack of magazines from under the counter. 'I hope you don't mind, dear, but I started a couple of the crosswords. With Clyde away visiting his mother, I've no one to talk to and it's been rather dull in the evenings. I don't for the life of me know how you finish the whole things. I can't understand some of those clues at all. I've earmarked all the competitions too.'

Mrs Mogg had also benefitted from Clarissa's good luck. When Mrs Mogg's refrigerator broke down, Lady Clarissa won an entire white goods package, which, having just won a remodelled kitchen for Penberthy House, Clarissa didn't need at all.

Clementine was standing in the far aisle looking at the ribbons Mrs Mogg had recently got into the shop. There was a very pretty pale blue one that she was hoping to add to her collection.

She wandered back to where her mother was sorting through the letters. Clementine noticed that there were lots of the ones with the red writing in the corner. They always seemed to make her mother frown.

Clarissa stopped at one with handwriting that was all swirly and curly.

Margaret Mogg watched from the other side of the counter as Clarissa opened the letter and began to read.

Clarissa caught her breath. 'Oh no.'

'Is everything all right, dear?' Mrs Mogg enquired.

'No, not really. Not at all. Aunt Violet is coming to stay,' Clarissa gulped.

'Oh dear.' Mrs Mogg frowned, recalling all

too well the last time Violet Appleby had visited the village. The woman had run up a hefty bill at the store and left her niece to pay for it.

'Who's Aunt Violet?' Clemmie asked.

'She's your grandfather's sister and she's positively horrid and I rather hoped never to see her again after the last time,' said Clarissa. She was looking very pale.

'Is she on the wall?' Clementine asked, referring to the family portraits that hung all over Penberthy House. She couldn't remember her mother ever mentioning anyone called Violet before.

'Yes, two along from your grandfather, on the stairs,' Clarissa replied.

'Oh, she's beautiful, Mummy!' Clementine exclaimed. 'But I call her Grace because you never told me her name.'

'There is nothing gracious about that woman,' Clarissa muttered under her breath to Mrs Mogg and then glanced down at her daughter. 'And remember, Clemmie, that portrait was painted about fifty years ago.'

Clementine wondered what her mother meant.

'When's she coming?' Mrs Mogg asked.

'According to this letter, she'll be here tomorrow afternoon,' Clarissa said. 'We'd better get home.'

'Why don't you like her, Mummy?' Clementine asked.

'It's complicated,' her mother replied. 'She wasn't always mean. In fact, when I was little she was bags of fun. But there were some unfortunate incidents and her horridness has grown on her, a bit like barnacles.'

Barnacles! Clementine had never seen a person with barnacles. Uncle Digby had shown her barnacles clinging to the side of some boats when they went on a trip to the seaside. And they were all over the pier too. But on people? That sounded terrible.

'Hold on a tick.' Mrs Mogg disappeared through the door behind the counter, which led to the kitchen and the flat behind. 'Take this,' she called, returning with a chocolate sponge cake that was beautifully decorated with fresh strawberries. 'Pierre dropped it in this morning on his way through the village and I don't need a whole sponge to myself.' She patted her round tummy.

'Thank you, Margaret. That's wonderful,' Clarissa said. 'I won't have time to bake a thing this afternoon. Come on, Clemmie, we need to hurry.'

'Is Aunt Violet really covered in seashells?' Clementine asked her mother. She'd been thinking about the barnacles for the last few minutes.

Clarissa looked at her daughter quizzically. 'Whatever do you mean, Clementine?'

'You said that her horridness was like barnacles,' Clementine replied.

'Oh, Clemmie, I didn't mean it like that. It's just an expression. She wasn't always mean but the meanness has built up over the years, a bit like the way barnacles grow on boats and things when they're left in the water too long.' Clarissa smiled tightly and shook her

head. 'I didn't mean to frighten you, darling. Aunt Violet may be a lot of things but she's not covered in seashells.'

Phew! Clementine was glad to hear it.

Margaret Mogg smiled at the pair. 'Don't you worry yourself, Clementine. I'm sure Aunt Violet will be perfectly well behaved. And don't fret, dear,' she said, looking at Clarissa. 'If she wants to buy anything this time, it will be cash only.'

Clarissa raised her eyebrows, gathered up the mail and placed it in her basket. Mrs Mogg packaged up the sponge in a cake box and put it into a carry bag.

'Thank you, Margaret,' Clarissa sighed.

'Bye, Mrs Mogg,' Clemmie called as she followed her mother quickly out of the shop. 'Bye, Claws,' she called to the sleeping tabby. 'Come on, Lavender.' She gathered up the lead and the little pig skittered to her feet and followed behind her.

AUNT VIOLET

Clementine had been wondering about Aunt Violet and the unfortunate incidents all afternoon. Maybe her mother had accidentally spilled orange juice on her, like Clementine had on one of the guests at breakfast last week. It wasn't Clemmie's fault that the lady was wearing a white pants-suit, and Clemmie was only trying to help because Uncle Digby was busy in the kitchen. Maybe her mother had accidentally snapped the key in the lock of the bathroom door when Aunt

Violet was in there, as Clementine had done to another guest a few weeks before. That lady wasn't happy at all when Uncle Digby had to climb up a ladder and go through the bathroom window to rescue her.

Clementine loved being a good helper. It was just that sometimes things didn't work out the way she planned. She wondered if her mother had been like that too when she was younger.

On the way home from the village she had asked her mother lots of questions about Aunt Violet. But Lady Clarissa was too lost in her own thoughts to give Clemmie the answers she wanted.

When they got back to the house, two of their guests had already arrived. While her mother and Uncle Digby were busy fussing over them, Clementine was left to play on her own with Lavender. She was practising with her skipping rope on the front lawn and Lavender was munching on some long grass near the stone wall when a shiny red car roared up the driveway. Clementine knew it was an expensive one, too, because it had a big silver star on the bonnet. Uncle Digby was always saying that if he won the lottery he would buy one just like it.

Clementine ran over to say hello. She liked greeting the guests and her mother said that it was important to be friendly and make a good impression. A very thin, tall woman with the most perfect silver bobbed hairdo got out of the car. She wore a stylish lime green pants-suit and Clementine noticed her matching shoes. Her huge sunglasses were round and dark and she didn't take them off.

The woman looked at the house and shuddered.

'Hello,' said Clementine. 'I like your shoes. Are you staying here?'

'Yes,' the woman replied. 'What are *you* doing here?' She raised her glasses to the top of her head and narrowed her dark-blue eyes as she studied the child in her pretty dress.

'I live here,' Clementine replied.

The woman glared at her. 'What do you mean you live here? Since when?'

'Since I came with the dinner rolls,' Clementine answered truthfully.

'Since you came with the dinner rolls! What sort of an answer is that?' the woman scoffed. 'Do you know where the lady of the house is?'

'Well, I'm not really sure because Mummy's been running around taking care of some of the other guests. She's been upset ever since we were in the village this morning and she found out that her Aunt Violet is coming tomorrow. I've never met her. She has a beautiful portrait on the stairs and I talk to her quite a bit, except that I call her Grace because I didn't know her real name. But Mummy says that she's horrid and she's like a barnacle. She must be very old too, I think,' Clementine gabbled.

The woman's eyes seemed to change colour from blue to black right in front of Clementine.

She stared at the child.

She leaned closer.

She pointed one finger right in front of Clementine's nose.

And just as she was about to speak, the front door of the house opened and Lady Clarissa raced out onto the driveway.

'Oh, Aunt Violet, you're early. It's good to see you,' she gushed, kissing the woman on both cheeks.

'Really?' Violet straightened her back and arched her perfectly plucked left eyebrow at Clarissa. 'You're glad to see me? That's not what I've just heard. And I told you I'd be here on Friday.'

Clarissa fingered the letter in her pocket. She knew it said Saturday, but there was no point arguing with Aunt Violet.

Clementine was biting her lip. Sometimes she wished she didn't talk so much.

'Clemmie, come and meet your Great-aunt Violet,' Clarissa instructed.

'Oh, we've met,' Violet snarled. 'But when did you have a baby, Clarissa?'

'But I told you before, Aunt Violet, I came with

the dinner rolls,' said Clementine. She wondered if her great-aunt had a hearing problem.

Clarissa began to explain. 'It's complicated –'

'Of course it's complicated. It's never simple with you, dear, is it? Now, are you going to ask me in or do I have to stand out here for the rest of the afternoon?' asked Violet tightly.

'Of course, Aunt Violet, the kettle's on and I've got a lovely chocolate sponge.' Clarissa turned and frowned at Clementine. Clemmie had never seen her mother like this before. 'This way,' said Clarissa and walked back towards the house.

'I need to get Pharaoh,' Violet snapped. She strode around to the passenger side of the car and opened the door. She pulled out a rectangular black bag, and headed for the front door.

Clementine noticed that the bag had mesh on both ends. 'What's Pharaoh?' she asked, peering into the mesh.

The occupant of the bag hissed.

Clementine recoiled. 'I hope he's not a snake. Mummy hates snakes and last week I got into big trouble for leaving my python in one of the bedrooms.'

'He's a sphynx,' Violet replied. She glared at the little girl. 'And he doesn't like children. Do you, my gorgeous little man?'

Clementine tried to get a closer look. She'd never seen a sphynx before.

'I suppose I have to show myself inside then, do I, seeing that niece of mine has vanished,' Violet tutted.

'I can take you.' Clementine walked beside the woman. 'And I'm sorry about what I said, Aunt Violet. I didn't recognise you. You're much older than the lady on the wall near Grandpa.'

'Don't apologise,' said Violet tartly. 'In my experience most people don't usually mean it when they say sorry, and as you're just a child, I don't imagine that you ever mean it.'

Violet strode into the hall, leaving Clementine on the front steps wondering what she had meant. Clementine *was* sorry. She didn't know why Aunt Violet didn't believe her.

PIG
TALES

Clementine Rose called Lavender to come inside. As soon as she heard her name the little pig ran towards her and the two of them headed off to find her mother.

'Hello Uncle Digby,' Clementine said, as she almost bumped into him. He just managed to steady the tea tray he was carrying.

'Ooh, ooh, careful, Clementine. Good afternoon, Lavender. Your mother tells me Aunt Violet has arrived a day early. I'm afraid it's not

35

a surprise. She never was very reliable. Have you met her yet?' the old man asked.

'Yes, just a little while ago. I think I said the wrong thing,' Clementine said with a worried frown.

'My dear girl, no one ever says the right thing to that woman,' the butler said with a smile. 'But don't worry. We haven't seen her in years and I suspect that as soon as she's upset your mother to her satisfaction, she'll be off and we won't see her again for another ten years. I'd best get this tea to the guests in the front sitting room. Your mother is in the kitchen.'

'She's got a sphynx,' Clementine informed him.

Digby frowned. He looked at Clementine patiently and waited for her to explain further.

'It's in a bag and it hissed at me,' Clementine said. 'I hope it's not dangerous.'

Digby hoped so too.

Clementine skipped off to the kitchen with Lavender tripping along behind her. Lady

Clarissa was pulling teacups and their matching saucers down from the dresser.

'Hello Mummy,' the child said as she and Lavender entered the room. 'Where's Aunt Violet?'

'Upstairs.' Clarissa turned and Clementine noticed she was frowning. 'I had planned to put her in the Blue Room on the third floor but she insisted on having the Rose Room on the second with the bathroom attached. I'd kept that for the guests arriving this evening. I can't possibly charge the same rate for the other room. It's much smaller and not nearly as nice.' She bit her lip. 'And now the guests will have to share their bathroom, which they specifically asked not to.'

'Mummy, why don't you like Aunt Violet?' Clementine Rose asked as she pulled out a chair and sat at the kitchen table. Lavender lay down underneath and settled in for a snooze.

'It's a very long story but she was horrible to Grandpa and to me.'

'What about?' Clementine asked.

'Money,' her mother replied as she fetched the teapot from the stove.

'But we don't have any, so we don't have to worry about it,' Clementine said. She'd heard her mother say that to Uncle Digby lots of times.

Clarissa laughed. 'Yes, and I suppose that's the problem. Aunt Violet and your grandfather fought about money. You see, he inherited Penberthy House from his parents and Aunt Violet got a small allowance and nothing more.'

'But why didn't she get the house too?' Clementine asked.

'That's just how things worked then, I'm afraid. The eldest son got the house. But Grandpa and Aunt Violet had been very close when they were children and he always felt badly about it too, so over the years he gave Aunt Violet as much as he could. He even bought her a cottage so she'd have a home but Aunt Violet sold everything to pay for her expensive clothes and holidays.'

Clementine still looked confused.

'Your great-aunt likes the finer things in life,' her mother explained. 'But you don't need to worry about any of it, Clementine. I'm hoping that she'll be gone tomorrow.'

'I thought Grandpa looked a bit annoyed,' said Clementine, nodding.

'Did you think so, darling?' her mother asked fondly.

'Oh yes, he looked cross when I came inside,' the child said.

The walls in Penberthy House were lined with portraits of all the past owners and family members. A large painting of Clemmie's grandfather hung in the entrance hall, along with one of her grandmother and, she now knew, Aunt Violet. Clementine liked to talk to them from time to time, and was certain that they changed their expressions depending on what was going on around the house. She was sure that her grandmother laughed the first time Lavender tried to walk up the stairs and kept on slipping back down. Her grandfather had a kindly smile and Clementine often chatted to him about this and that. She liked to practise her poems for them as well. Lady Clarissa would often hear her daughter telling tales to the family. She thought it was wonderful that Clementine had such a vivid imagination.

The clacking of heels on the bare timber floor rang out a warning that someone was approaching.

'Is the tea ready yet?' Violet's voice entered the room before she did.

'Won't be a moment, Aunt Violet,' Clarissa said quickly and busied herself pouring boiling water into the teapot.

Clementine looked at her great-aunt. She wondered what had happened to the beautiful young woman in the portrait.

Violet stared back at Clementine.

'Am I to take tea in here? In the kitchen?' the old woman scoffed. 'While your friends are waited on hand and foot in the sitting room?'

Clarissa ignored Violet's questions and

placed a teacup and plate with a large slice of sponge cake on the table.

Violet stared at the tea and cake. 'Well, I suppose that's your answer.' She pulled out a chair and sat down. 'Is this Mother's good china?' The older woman lifted the plate and studied the underside.

'Yes, Aunt Violet,' Clarissa replied. 'I'm afraid I've had to use what we've got over the years. I can't afford to replace it.'

'This was only ever allowed out of the cupboard on Christmas Day. Mother would turn in her grave.' The woman shook her head. 'I should have taken it and sold it when I had the chance,' she whispered under her breath.

'Do you have milk, Aunt Violet?' Clarissa asked, hoping to steer her off the subject of the china.

'Of course I do. I should think you'd remember, Clarissa,' Violet snarled. She pointed at the cake. 'Did you make that?'

'No, I'm afraid not,' Clarissa said. 'I haven't had time today.'

'Pierre made it,' Clementine offered. 'He makes the best cakes ever.'

Violet tilted her chin upwards and gave Clementine a sidelong glance. 'We'll see about that.'

'Would you like to hear a poem?' Clementine asked.

'A what?' Violet sipped her tea.

'A poem,' Clementine replied. 'I know lots of them by heart and I have some funny ones too.'

'No, not particularly. In fact, I'd rather that you left the room,' Violet snapped. 'I need to speak to your mother. In private.'

'But Lavender's asleep,' said Clementine seriously.

'Who's Lavender? Don't tell me there's another child I don't know about?' Violet asked.

'Lavender's my pig,' Clementine said. 'She's a teacup.'

The woman's eyes widened and she stared at the teacup in her hand. 'You have a dirty, smelly pig? And it's called Lavender?'

'Pigs aren't dirty or smelly, Aunt Violet. Pigs

are smart and cuddly. Lavender's only as big as a cat, and she won't grow any more,' Clementine replied. 'That's why she's called a teacup pig.'

'What a load of nonsense,' Violet scoffed. 'I've never heard such tripe. Everyone knows that pigs are huge and disgusting and they live outside in sties. Off you go. Your mother and I need to talk. About you, among other things.'

'Aunt Violet, please don't speak to my daughter like that.' Clarissa spoke in a voice barely more than a whisper.

'But I can't go,' said Clementine with a scowl. 'I told you already. Lavender's asleep.' She was becoming more certain that her great-aunt was hard of hearing.

'Where is this so-called teacup pig?' asked Violet. 'I suppose you keep it in the kitchen, do you?'

'She's under my chair,' Clementine replied.

Aunt Violet gasped. She looked towards Clarissa, who nodded, then back at Clementine. The child pointed under her chair. Violet knelt down to look. Clementine Rose knelt down at

43

the other end of the table. Their eyes locked underneath.

'There she is,' Clementine whispered, and pointed. 'Please don't wake her up because she's very tired.' She put her finger to her lips.

Violet settled back into her chair.

'What sort of circus are you running here, Clarissa?' the old woman demanded. 'First a child, then a pig in the house and those friends of yours in the sitting room had the hide to ask me if I could get them some more soap for their bathroom – what do I look like? The hired help?' Violet placed her teacup on the table with a thud.

'I can explain,' Clarissa began.

Digby Pertwhistle entered the room, carrying the tea tray full of dirty cups and saucers. 'Good afternoon, Miss Appleby,' Digby said with a nod towards her. 'Welcome back to Penberthy House.'

'I can't believe that *you're* still here. I thought you'd have shuffled off years ago,' the woman snarled.

'And it's lovely to see you too.' Digby winked at Clementine as he went to the sink and began to unpack the tray.

'The place is falling down around your ears, Clarissa, and you still insist on having Pertwhistle here,' Violet hissed. 'I can't imagine how you pay the man.'

'Mummy wins things,' Clementine said.

Clarissa had hoped Clementine wouldn't bring that subject up.

'What do you mean?' Violet demanded.

'Mummy wins lots of competitions. She won that coffee machine and this whole kitchen and new beds for upstairs and even a holiday to Tahiti that Uncle Digby took last year,' Clementine explained. 'She won Lavender at the fair too, which was very lucky because teacup pigs cost a lot of money.'

'Well, aren't you just the fortunate one, Clarissa,' Violet said through pursed lips.

'How long are you staying, Aunt Violet?' Clementine asked.

'I haven't decided,' the woman replied.

Lady Clarissa and Digby Pertwhistle looked at each other, horrified at the thought of having to put up with the woman for any longer than a night.

'Mummy's very good at looking after people,' Clementine announced.

Clarissa and Digby gulped in unison. It was another of those times they both wished Clementine wasn't quite so honest.

'Clementine, why don't you take Lavender upstairs and put her in her basket?' her mother suggested. 'I'm sure you can do that without waking her up.'

Clementine peeked at the sleepy pig. Digby lifted the chair and Clementine picked her up, cradling her like a baby.

'That's the most ridiculous thing I've ever seen in my life,' Violet huffed, then shooed Clementine as if waving away a pesky fly. 'Well, hurry up then, off you go.'

When Aunt Violet wasn't looking, Clementine wrinkled her nose at the beastly woman.

THE SPHYNX

Clementine Rose carried the dozing pig upstairs to her bedroom and laid her in her basket. Lavender stirred and grunted a couple of times but Clemmie tickled her tummy and soon she was fast asleep.

Clementine spent some time colouring in and practising the new poem Uncle Digby had taught her but after a while she felt fidgety.

She noticed that the house had fallen quiet. Usually that meant the guests were off on a ramble or having a rest in their rooms.

She kept thinking about Aunt Violet. The lady in the painting was much nicer to talk to than the woman downstairs. *She* was a bossy boots.

Then Clementine remembered the sphynx. Aunt Violet was staying downstairs on the second floor in the Rose Room. She left Lavender sound asleep and made her way along the hall and down the main staircase to the level below. The Rose Room was by far the biggest and prettiest in the whole house. It was also the one that her mother used to advertise the hotel. The room was at the end of the corridor and had a wonderful view of the garden on three sides. It was also the only room with a new bathroom, which had been installed after Lady Clarissa won a bathroom makeover package the year before.

Clementine knocked at the door. There was no answer so she turned the handle and opened it just enough to peek her head around.

'Hello, Aunt Violet, are you here?' she called. The room was silent.

Clementine looked about for the black bag. Uncle Digby must have brought up Aunt Violet's luggage from the car. Sitting on the floor at the end of the bed were three huge suitcases and a beauty case as well. Clementine thought that was a lot for someone staying just one night. Usually weekend guests had only half as much.

One of the suitcases was open. Clementine had a peek under the flap. Sitting on top of a pile of neatly folded clothes was a small gold clock and a bronze statue of a horse. There were some silver candlesticks too. She thought Aunt Violet must really like those things a lot to take them with her for a holiday.

A ruby velvet chaise longue sat underneath the side window. The fabric was a little frayed around the edges but Lady Clarissa had a clever way with throw rugs and cushions and could make the shabbiest of furniture seem well loved rather than in need of fixing. A tall cedar chest of drawers stood beside the doorway to the ensuite bathroom. A roll-top writing desk took up one corner of the room, and there was a dressing table too. On it sat a large vase full of red, pink and peach roses her mother had cut from the garden.

Clementine's favourite thing in the Rose Room was the enormous four-poster bed. It was so tall that you needed a special stepladder to climb onto it. When the house was empty, Clementine often spent time in this room, climbing up and down onto the bed. Lavender tried to get up too sometimes but her little legs just weren't long enough.

Clementine tiptoed around to the other side of the bed.

'Sphynx,' she whispered in a singsong voice, 'where are you?' Then she spotted the black bag sitting open on the floor. 'Oh!' Clementine gasped. The bag was empty. Maybe the creature was on the bed. She scooted up the little ladder onto the patchwork duvet and came face to face with the strangest creature she'd ever seen.

'Argh!' She drew in a sharp breath and kept

as still as she could. It was lying in the middle of the bed and had huge pointy ears and a strange wrinkly head. The beast half-opened its green eyes and glared at her.

Clementine had no idea what it was. It sort of looked like a giant rat or maybe a cat, but it didn't have any fur. The creature stared at her in a disgusted sort of way, just like the lady had looked at her when she had spilled the orange juice the week before.

Clementine gulped.

'What are you doing in here?' a voice demanded. Clementine Rose spun around to see Aunt Violet charging through the door. 'You leave my Pharaoh alone,' she growled.

'I . . . I didn't touch him, I promise,' Clementine protested.

'I told you before that he doesn't like children.' Violet strode towards the bed, her eyes scanning the room. 'Have you been snooping through my things?'

Clementine shook her head. 'No, of course not, Aunt Violet. Well, except that I saw your horse statue and some candlesticks and a clock. They must be very precious for you to bring them on holidays.'

'You little sneak.' Violet glimpsed the official-looking document poking out of the top of her handbag. The first words were: 'Eviction Notice'. She walked over and stuffed it back inside, wondering if Clementine could yet read.

Clementine gulped.

'Well, you shouldn't be in here,' Violet snapped.

'What . . . what is he?' Clementine asked.

'What's who?' Violet replied.

'Him.' Clementine pointed at the creature on the bed.

'He's a sphynx,' the old woman replied, rolling her eyes. 'I told you that earlier. Or are your ears full of wax?'

'No, Mummy cleans my ears every Thursday at bath time, except if I'm too tired and I don't have a bath, and then she does it on Friday,' Clementine said. 'I know he's a sphynx but what sort of creature is that?'

'It's a cat, of course, you silly child,' said Violet, shaking her head.

Clementine had never seen a cat like it before and she knew quite a few. There was Claws at the village shop and her friend Sophie had a fluffy white kitten called Mintie. Her other friend Poppy had lots of cats on the farm at Highton Hall and none of them looked even the slightest bit like Pharaoh.

'Is something wrong with him?' Clementine asked.

'Of course not.' Violet reached into the middle of the bed and patted the cat's wrinkly head.

'But . . .' Clementine wondered if she should tell Aunt Violet what she could see. Maybe the woman had something wrong with her eyesight as well as her hearing. Clementine decided that it was better to tell the truth. 'He's got no hair.'

'He was born that way,' Violet replied, as if it was the most usual thing in the world to have a bald cat. 'My *bootiful* boy.' Violet leaned across the bed and nuzzled against his face. The cat hissed at her.

Clementine wondered if Aunt Violet had taken him to the vet to see if there was a cure. Pharaoh was just about the ugliest creature she'd ever seen, apart from Father Bob's dribbly bulldog, Adrian.

'And what are you doing in my room, anyway?' Violet asked, glaring at Clementine.

The child gulped. She seemed to be asked that question quite a lot. 'I wanted to see what a sphynx was,' she replied.

'Well, now you have and I would thank you to stay out of *my* room, young lady.' Violet walked to the door and held it open.

Clementine slid down from the bed and walked towards her.

Violet stared at the child with her pretty blonde hair and ink-blue eyes. There was something vaguely familiar about her, yet the woman knew that was impossible. She'd never heard of her before today, let alone seen her.

'Off you go,' said Violet. 'I have things to do, and talking to you is not one of them.'

Clementine smiled at the old woman.

She had a habit of doing that when she was nervous.

'What are you grinning about?' Violet demanded.

'Nothing, Aunt Violet, nothing at all,' said Clementine, and scurried out the door.

A HAIRY
STORY

After her visit with Pharaoh and Aunt Violet, Clementine Rose decided to find her mother and Uncle Digby and warn them about the bald sphynx. She wondered if they might have some ideas about a cure.

Clementine was on her way to the kitchen when she was distracted by a man. She heard him before she saw him – the loudest grunting snores ever. That was saying something because there had been plenty of snorers taking naps in the sitting room over the years. When she reached the bottom of the stairs she saw him in the winged armchair by the fireplace, with his head tilted back and his mouth wide open.

Clementine decided to take a closer look. She tiptoed into the room and stood beside the chair, resting her elbows on the arm with her head cradled in her hands. She thought he must be quite old. His forehead and cheeks were lined like crinkle-cut chips, and the skin on his neck hung loose, just like on the turkey Mr Mogg was keeping before last Christmas.

His hands were resting in his lap and she noticed they had lots of tan spots on them. Clementine liked watching the way the long hairs that stuck out of his nostrils fluttered in time with his breaths.

She glanced up at his hair. Most of the older men Clementine knew had grey or silver hair, like Mr Mogg and Father Bob, or not very much at all, like Uncle Digby. He just had a few long strands that he combed over the top and kept in place with some goo from a jar. This man's hair was dark orange and there was something not quite right about the way it was sitting. Clementine stood up on her tippy-toes and reached out to touch the thick crop. Her finger pressed against it gently. The man snorted loudly and she jumped back. Clemmie held her breath but his eyes stayed firmly shut. She wanted to touch his hair again – it felt rough, like the soap pad Uncle Digby used to scrub the saucepans. She reached up and stretched out her hand but just as she did, something terrible happened. As she made contact with the hair, it slid right off the top of his head and onto the floor.

Clemmie clutched her hands to her mouth. She'd never seen anyone's hair fall off like that before. The orange mop lay on the floor like a flat ginger cat. Clementine leaned down to get a closer look. She didn't want to touch it any more but somehow she had to get it back on top of the man's head.

Clementine gripped it between her pointer

finger and thumb and lifted it up slowly. Just as the hair was level with the top of the man's head, a fly began to buzz around his left ear. And right at the same time Clementine was about to deposit the hair back onto his head, the man stirred and swatted at the fly. He missed and flicked his hair right into the fireplace, where it erupted into flames and burnt away to nothing in seconds.

Clementine stood perfectly still and held her breath. She wondered if she could make him some new hair and tape it to his shiny head before he woke up. She remembered her old toy orangutan. Then she remembered that she'd lost it at her friend Poppy's house.

Maybe the man wouldn't notice. Maybe he had some more hair in his suitcase that he could wear instead. Maybe it would grow back before he woke up.

Clementine was staring at the man and wondering what to do, when out of the corner of her eye she saw a reflection of something moving in the mirror above the fireplace. It was just a flash but she knew that there was someone else in the room. The sitting room was shaped like a capital 'L', with another entrance from the back hallway. Clementine wondered if whoever it was had seen what happened with the man and his hair.

She decided to see who was there and tiptoed past the long floral sofa and the china cabinet to investigate. Clementine leaned around the corner in slow motion.

'Oh!' she gasped. Sticking up in the air was a bottom and it was attached to Aunt Violet. The old woman was down on her hands and knees with her head under the green velvet grandfather chair.

Clementine watched for a moment.

'Hello Aunt Violet,' she whispered.

There was a dull thud as Violet thwacked her head on the underside of the chair.

'Ow!' the woman grumbled as she wriggled out. 'You again!'

'Have you lost something?' Clementine asked.

'No, of course not.' Violet stood up and smoothed the front of her trousers. 'Have you?' She arched an eyebrow menacingly.

Clementine wondered if Aunt Violet had seen what happened to the man and his hair. She shook her head slowly.

She knew that she should tell the truth. It was just that, at the moment, she didn't quite know how. And after all, it was an accident.

Aunt Violet looked at Clementine and sniffed. Then she turned on her heel and strode out of the room.

Clementine tiptoed back towards the man without the hair. He was still fast asleep. She decided that the best plan was to find Uncle Digby and tell him the truth. He would know what to do.

TRUTH
TIME

Clementine Rose found Digby Pertwhistle in the dining room, setting
the huge mahogany table for dinner.

'Hello Clemmie,' he said. 'What have you
been up to now?'

Clementine gulped. She wondered if Uncle
Digby had special powers. He always seemed
to know when there was trouble about.

'Nothing much,' she replied, not quite ready
to talk about the burnt hair. 'I met Aunt Violet's
sphynx.'

'Oh, yes, and what sort of a creature is this sphynx?' Digby asked.

'Aunt Violet says that he's a cat but he's the strangest looking cat I've ever seen. He's got no hair,' Clementine explained. 'But I don't think she can see that.'

Digby considered this. 'Interesting.'

'He's not interesting,' Clementine replied. 'He's ugly.'

'Perhaps he has a special personality,' said Digby.

Clementine shook her head. 'I don't think so. He even hissed at Aunt Violet.'

'Sounds like a smart cat if you ask me,' said Digby, his lips twitching. He continued putting the cutlery in place.

'Uncle Digby, I need to tell you something,' said Clementine. She took a small step closer to the man, then another, until she stood right beside him.

He turned and bent down to meet her gaze. 'Uh-oh. What have you done now, Clementine?'

'Well,' she began, 'I didn't mean to but it just sort of happened.'

'I have to get some wine from the cellar,' said Digby. 'Why don't you come with me and you can explain on the way.'

Clementine nodded.

On the evenings they had guests, Clementine, her mother and Digby Pertwhistle usually ate in the kitchen before the meal was served. But tonight Clarissa wasn't quite sure what to do. Aunt Violet wasn't a paying guest but she was expecting to be served in the dining room.

After his visit to the cellar with Clementine, Digby Pertwhistle was as puzzled by what to do about the man and his missing hair as Clementine was.

She hadn't realised exactly how tricky a subject hair was. When her mother told her that they would be eating in the dining room with Aunt Violet and the guests, Clementine

asked if she could have dinner with Uncle Digby instead.

'No, Clemmie,' her mother replied. 'I need you to be charming to everyone and hopefully Aunt Violet will behave herself. Digby, I hope you don't mind serving all of us tonight.'

'Of course not, my dear. Although perhaps if you made Violet eat her dinner out here in the kitchen with us as we usually do, she might pack her bags and head for home,' Digby suggested.

'I had thought of that,' said Clarissa, 'but I don't want her making a fuss and upsetting the guests, which she's sure to do if we leave her out here. She still doesn't know that we run the house as a hotel. She's such a terrible snob. I can't imagine she'll be pleased when she finds out. Mrs Mogg is coming to help with dinner so I can look after Aunt Violet. And I *still* don't know why she's here. She won't give me a straight answer.'

'Maybe she wants to make up and be friends,' Clementine suggested. 'And give you a present. She has lots of things in her suitcase.'

'*How* do you know what she has in her suitcase?' asked Clarissa, casting her daughter a stern look. 'I hope you haven't been snooping, young lady.'

Clementine shook her head. 'I went to visit her and her bag was open and she has candlesticks and a clock and even a bronze statue of a horse.'

'Really? Why would she bring all of that with her?' Clarissa bit her lip and looked thought-ful, then shook herself and said, 'Anyway, Clementine, run along and put on a fresh dress and then come straight back down to the dining room. And no more spying.'

Clementine nodded. 'I'm going to wear my green stripes with the pink cardigan. Can Lavender come too?'

'Oh no, Clemmie, not tonight. Make sure that she has a fresh bowl of water and her litter box is clean and I'll take her up some pellets,' her mother instructed. 'I don't think Lavender would improve Aunt Violet's mood at all.'

The child skipped off up the back stairs that led from the kitchen to the upper levels. She opened her bedroom door and found Lavender pushing a little ball all over the floor. The pig squealed when she saw her mistress.

'Hello Lavender.' Clementine gave the tiny pig a scratch on the top of her head. 'Sorry, but Mummy says you have to stay up here tonight. We've got to eat dinner with the guests in the dining room and I'm scared about seeing the man from the sitting room,' she explained to the pig, who had scrambled into her lap and was enjoying a rub on her grey belly. 'I think Aunt Violet's going to tell on me.'

Lavender grunted and closed her eyes.

'I told Uncle Digby what happened and he said that perhaps we should just wait and see. But I don't know what we're waiting for and I already know what we'll see. That man is as bald as Aunt Violet's cat. I haven't told you about him, have I? He's very strange,' said Clementine, looking at Lavender's pink tummy. 'I suppose you don't really have much

71

hair either,' she observed, 'but you're a pig and you're not meant to have hair. Cats are.'

Clementine placed Lavender back on the floor and checked the water bowl and litter box, which was over in the corner of the room behind a screen. Then she took her green striped dress from the wardrobe and changed.

'Be good, Lavender, and I'll bring you some vegetables.' Clementine pulled on her cardigan and sat down to buckle her pink shoes.

Lavender grunted and waddled over to her basket.

'I'll see you after dinner.' Clementine quickly ran a brush through her hair and found a green hairclip to pin back the sweep of blonde hair that covered her eyes. 'There.'

A NIGHT TO REMEMBER

The guests were gathered in the dining room by the time Clementine arrived. Her mother was chatting away while Uncle Digby offered champagne. Aunt Violet hadn't yet appeared.

'Clementine, come and meet everyone,' her mother instructed. There were two couples and a single lady staying in the house. 'This is Mr and Mrs O'Connell.' Clarissa nodded at a man wearing a smart sports coat and his wife, who wore a lovely tangerine-coloured silk shirt with white pants. 'This is my daughter, Clementine Rose,' Clarissa told them.

'Hello there, Clementine Rose,' the man said. 'Aren't you a lucky girl to live in a lovely big house like this?'

'Hello,' Clementine smiled. 'Yes, but I wish it didn't have so many holes in the roof.'

Mr and Mrs O'Connell exchanged quizzical looks.

'Come along, darling, and meet our other guests.' Clarissa guided Clementine away. She introduced her to a younger woman with long dark hair. 'This is Miss Herring. She's writing a book, Clementine, isn't that exciting?'

'Hello,' Clementine said. 'Does it have lots of pictures? I can't read yet but I'm going to big school soon and then I'll be able to.'

'No, I'm afraid that it doesn't have any pictures at all,' Miss Herring replied. 'It's about business.'

Clementine wrinkled her nose. 'It sounds a bit . . . boring,' she whispered.

'Clementine, I'm sure Miss Herring's book is wonderful,' her mother rebuked.

Miss Herring smiled thinly.

'Now, Clementine, I want you to meet Mr and Mrs Sparks.' Clarissa took Clemmie's hand and led her to the other side of the room.

Clementine gulped. The man and woman appeared to be having an argument, except that it was all whispers and his face looked red and cross.

'Oh, for heaven's sake, Floyd, I've told you a thousand times that no one stole your wretched hairpiece and if they did, I'd have to find them and thank them for getting rid of the ridiculous thing anyway,' the woman said, rolling her eyes.

'Is everything all right?' Clarissa asked.

'Yes, my dear. Floyd's lost his toupee and he thinks someone must have stolen it while he was having a nap this afternoon. I can't imagine for one second who would want to steal it – it was quite revolting and I've been telling him for years that he looks much better without it,' Mrs Sparks explained.

Clementine stood beside her mother, wondering if she should say anything.

'And who do we have here?' asked Mrs Sparks, as she looked at Clementine.

'This is my daughter, Clementine Rose,' Clarissa said.

'Hello dear, it's a pleasure to meet you and I must say I love your dress,' said Mrs Sparks. She smiled at Clemmie, then dug her elbow into her husband's ribs.

'Oh hello,' the man said. 'You look like a smart girl. You didn't happen to see my hair anywhere this afternoon, did you?'

Clementine was just about to tell him what happened when Mrs Sparks interrupted them.

'Oh, Floyd Sparks, stop talking about that ridiculous rug. Clementine, dear, I hope the jolly thing ended up in the fire. He looks so much more handsome without it. It was orange, too. Can you believe a man of his age, wearing something so ridiculous? He hasn't had orange hair in years anyway. Jolly thing looked like a dead ginger cat on top of his head. Now tell me, Clementine, how old are you?'

'I'm five,' the child replied, trying not to smile. She was imagining a ginger cat sitting on top of Mr Sparks's head.

'How wonderful to be five,' Mrs Sparks enthused. 'You must tell me, what do five-year-olds like to get up to these days? I bet you must have lots of fun roaming about this big house of yours.'

'My friends are coming tomorrow to stay for the night,' Clementine said. 'And I'm going to ask Mummy if we can have a camp-out.'

'Oh my dear, that sounds wonderful,' Mrs Sparks nodded.

Lady Clarissa didn't comment. She was watching the door. 'Excuse me, Mr and Mrs Sparks, I see Aunt Violet has arrived,' she said. She made her way to the door where Violet was surveying the scene.

'You *do* have a rather strange group of friends, Clarissa,' the woman hissed.

'Come along, Aunt Violet, I've put you at the end of the table near Clementine and me.' Clarissa guided the woman into the room.

'I like your dress, Aunt Violet,' Clementine told the old woman. The print had circles in all different shades of green. Clementine liked the way it swirled around.

'Yes, it's lovely, isn't it?' said Violet. She looked at the child and couldn't help thinking her own selection of clothing was rather sweet too – although she wasn't about to tell her.

Digby Pertwhistle re-entered the room and asked that the guests be seated. He then walked around the table placing the napkins into each of the diner's laps.

'Aunt Violet, I'd like to introduce you to Edward and Sandra O'Connell,' said Clarissa, nodding towards the couple sitting opposite her aunt.

'Charmed, I'm sure,' Violet sneered.

'Hello,' the couple replied in unison.

'And this is Becca Herring,' Clarissa introduced the young woman, then turned to the couple at the end of the table. 'And Zelda and Floyd Sparks. This is my aunt, Violet Appleby.'

Violet frowned but said, 'Hello.' She looked the couple up and down. 'I saw you earlier this afternoon, Mr Sparks, but there's something different about you now.'

'He's lost his hair,' Zelda Sparks offered. 'And he looks all the better for it.'

'I see. And where did you lose your hair exactly?' Violet asked.

'Well, I was having a nap in the sitting room and then when I woke up it was gone,' Floyd explained.

Violet turned and stared at Clementine. 'Really? A nap in the sitting room, this afternoon?'

Clementine gulped.

'Never mind, Mr Sparks,' Violet said. 'I've always thought a man looks much better if he just lets nature take its course. And there is nothing quite as ridiculous as a man of a certain age trying to be something he's not.'

Floyd nodded sheepishly.

'Yes, Miss Appleby, I couldn't agree more,' Zelda Sparks replied. 'Now, tell me, do you live in this magnificent residence too?'

'No, Aunt Violet's just visiting,' Clementine said, smiling at her great-aunt.

'Oh look, here's the entree,' Lady Clarissa said hastily. She was wishing she'd served Aunt Violet dinner in the kitchen with the family. 'Tonight we have mushroom soup with sourdough bread.'

There was a murmur of approval around the table. Violet placed her spoon into the thick brown liquid and drew it to her lips. She was pleasantly surprised by the taste.

'How's Pharaoh?' Clementine asked her great-aunt.

The old woman looked down her nose at Clemmie. 'What?'

'Your cat? Is he feeling well?' Clementine said.

'How would I know?' Violet retorted. 'He can't speak, you know.'

'Lavender can't speak either but I always

know how she's feeling. When she's happy she runs around a lot and when she's sad she sits in her basket and rests her head on the side and she won't come when I call her. But that's only happened a couple of times. Once when Mrs Mogg's cat Claws scratched her on the nose, and one day when I had to leave her at home to have my "look-see" day at school,' Clementine explained.

Violet rolled her eyes at the child and turned to speak with Becca Herring.

Clementine stared at Aunt Violet's back and wrinkled her nose.

Digby cleared away the soup bowls and returned with the main course. He set the steaming plates down in front of each guest.

'Ooh, this looks lovely, Lady Clarissa,' exclaimed Floyd Sparks. His mood seemed to have improved vastly.

Clarissa smiled at her guest.

Clementine pushed her fork into the baked potato on her plate and swirled it in the thick gravy.

'Clemmie, remember your manners, please,' her mother tutted.

Clementine frowned. She hadn't forgotten her manners. She just wanted some gravy on her potato.

As the meal progressed, Violet couldn't help but wonder about her niece's friends. They didn't seem to know Clarissa very well at all.

'What a wonderful roast,' said Mr O'Connell as he finished the last bite of his lamb and placed his knife and fork together on the plate. 'We'll definitely be telling our friends about Penberthy House.'

Clarissa smiled thinly. 'Thank you, Mr O'Connell.'

'Why would you be telling your friends?' Violet asked.

'Well, your niece is quite the loveliest hostess and the wife and I haven't stayed in as nice a place as this for a long time. Although that bathroom upstairs could do with a bit of updating and I have noticed the wallpaper's falling down in a couple of spots.'

Violet glanced around the table. All of a sudden she realised exactly what was going on.

'Clarissa, I'd like a word. In private,' she said through clenched teeth.

Clarissa did her best to put the woman off. 'But Aunt Violet, we're about to have dessert.'

'And it's going to be yum, yum, yummy,' Clementine sang. 'Mrs Mogg made chocolate mousse and I love chocolate mousse.'

The rest of the group laughed.

'We won't be long.' Violet stood up and waited for Clarissa to do the same. The younger woman led the older one out of the dining room, along the hallway and into the library.

The library at Penberthy House held a magnificent collection of over ten thousand dusty, leather-bound books, some dating back hundreds of years. There was a fireplace and shelves from the floor to the ceiling, with a spiral staircase leading up to a balcony that ran around the top half of the room. A magnificent mahogany desk sat in the centre of the floor and there were old floral couches to sit on too, although most of them needed new springs and the covers were getting tatty.

Clarissa hoped that was far enough away that the guests wouldn't hear their conversation.

Violet closed the door and turned to her niece, blocking the way out. 'Clarissa, those people in there are not your friends.'

'No, Aunt Violet, they're not,' Clarissa replied.

'Well, what are they doing here?' the old woman demanded.

'They're staying for the weekend,' said Clarissa. She took a deep breath. 'So that I can keep Penberthy House.'

'So, all of those people are paying you to stay here?' Violet snapped.

'Yes, Aunt Violet. I've been running the house as a country hotel for years,' Clarissa replied. 'The repairs won't pay for themselves.'

'What happened to all that money your father left you?' Violet asked. 'He'd turn in his grave knowing you were renting the place to strangers.'

'There was only ever a little money, Aunt Violet, despite what you always thought. Father was a generous man and he had given away most of the family fortune. In fact, he gave a good deal of it to you. I'm sure that he never realised just how much it costs to look after this place,' Clarissa explained.

'You're telling me that Penberthy House is falling down because you can't afford to do any better?' Violet asked.

'Yes, there's no pot of gold,' Clarissa said firmly. 'And if you don't like what I'm doing then you can leave.'

'How dare you? I'm family. And I'll go when, and if, I'm ready,' Violet huffed. Her eyes darted around the room. 'What have you changed in here?' she demanded, still scanning the length and breadth of the library.

'Digby removed that horrid old cabinet that used to sit in front of the shelves at the end of the row, that's all.'

Violet walked towards the bookshelf. She drew in a sharp breath as if a memory had just

surfaced. 'Did he find anything behind it?' she asked.

'What do you mean?'

'Anything unusual?' Violet prompted.

Clarissa wondered what she was talking about. 'Just books and shelves. It always looked odd jutting out at the end and covering the row. It looks much better now, don't you think?'

'Yes, much better.' Violet smirked, then spun around and stalked off down the hallway towards the grand staircase.

Clarissa shook her head. Surely Aunt Violet wasn't planning to stay forever.

Meanwhile, back in the dining room, Digby Pertwhistle was serving dessert and Clementine Rose was entertaining the guests with one of her favourite poems. It was by a very famous man called Roald Dahl and it was about a crocodile.

She was imagining the crocodile had a face just like Aunt Violet's, but only half as mean.

The guests clapped loudly as she finished with a bow.

SLEEPOVER

By midday on Sunday the guests had all departed, except Aunt Violet, who had vanished after breakfast, leaving a trail of belongings strewn around the Rose Room.

Clementine was helping her mother take the sheets off the guest beds and wondering how long it would be until Sophie and Jules arrived. 'Where's Uncle Digby?' she asked.

'He's in the library. He said he wanted to give the place a spring clean,' Clarissa explained.

'Uncle Digby works hard, doesn't he, Mummy?' said Clementine.

'Yes, he does. We're lucky to have him,' her mother said with a nod.

'I've been thinking,' Clementine began.

'Uh-oh,' Clarissa smiled.

'It's nothing bad, Mummy. I was just wondering if we can have a camp-out tonight.'

Her mother frowned. 'But where do you want to camp this time?' When Clementine, Sophie and Jules last had a 'camp-out', it was in the front sitting room under a giant tent made from bedsheets, on a floor of cushions.

Clementine thought for a moment. They all liked camping in the Rose Room, where they could turn the four-poster bed into a giant tent. But that was off limits because Aunt Violet was there.

'Can we camp in the attic?' Clementine asked.

'No, Clemmie, it's jam-packed with all sorts of things and I think you might find it a little on the creepy side,' her mother replied. Clarissa didn't like going up there in the middle of the day, let alone the thought of staying there all night.

'What about the library?' Clementine suggested.

'Perfect,' her mother said. 'And at least there won't be any dust, either.'

Clementine loved the library. It was one of her favourite rooms in the whole house.

'Why don't you go and get some pillows from the linen press and take them downstairs,' her mother suggested. 'I can finish up here.'

Clementine nodded. 'Come on, Lavender,' she called to the tiny pig, who was snuffling about under the bed. 'We've got to get your basket and blanket and all the duvets and at least one hundred pillows.'

Clarissa smiled to herself. She couldn't imagine how dull her life would have been without Clementine.

Clementine dragged piles of pillows and duvets downstairs to the library where Digby Pertwhistle was almost finished cleaning.

After their second run, Lavender stayed behind and settled in for a nap under one of the armchairs.

As Clementine charged up the back stairs to her bedroom, she caught sight of Aunt Violet coming out of the room. She was tucking something sparkly into the pocket of her trousers.

'Hello Aunt Violet,' Clementine called. 'Were you looking for me?'

The old woman shot into the air and spun around.

'Good heavens, child, do you make a habit of sneaking up on people or do you reserve that especially for me?' she snarled.

'I didn't mean to.'

'Well, you did. And no, I wasn't looking *for you*,' Violet said with a small snort of disbelief.

'But you were in my room,' Clementine said, remembering how cross Aunt Violet had been when she had visited the Rose Room.

'It was *my* room, actually, when I was a girl. And I was just looking,' Violet replied.

'Did you like it?' Clementine asked.

'No, it was much prettier when it was mine. But I suppose we could always fix it up to the way it should be. Perhaps I'd like to have it again.'

'But it's *my* room now,' Clementine said.

'You could move,' said Violet. 'This is a big house.'

Clementine wondered what her great-aunt was talking about. She wasn't moving out of her room.

'Are you staying for a long time, Aunt Violet?' Clementine asked.

'That depends. Has Pertwhistle finished in the library yet?' the old woman demanded.

'No. Uncle Digby's doing a spring clean and they take ages and then my friends are coming to stay for the night and we're having a camp-out,' Clementine explained.

'What friends?' asked Violet.

'Sophie and Jules. They live in Highton Mill. Their father Pierre makes all of those lovely cakes you like to eat,' Clementine prattled.

'Village children?' Violet frowned. 'Don't you have any more suitable friends?'

Clementine was puzzled. 'I don't know what you mean, Aunt Violet.'

'I'm exhausted,' the woman declared. 'Tell your mother to bring me a cup of tea in my room. I've got a headache coming on.'

Clementine watched as her great-aunt strode along the hallway to the main staircase. Surely she couldn't take her room away. Grandpa would have something to say about that.

SOPHIE
AND JULES

'Now, make sure that you do everything Clarissa asks and don't get into any trouble,' Odette instructed her two children as they stood on the driveway beside Clementine and her mother.

'Come on, Odette, we 'ave to get all the way to Downsfordvale before dark,' Pierre called from the driver's seat.

Odette gave her children a kiss on each cheek and then did the same to Clementine and Clarissa.

'*Sacrebleu*, Odette, 'urry up. It's only for one night. We will come back and get them tomorrow. Maybe.' Pierre grinned and shrugged his shoulders.

'That's fine with us, Papa,' Jules told his father. 'We love it here.'

'Maybe your Mama and me, we'll leave you with Lady Clarissa for a week and take an 'oliday,' Pierre teased.

'We're having a camp-out,' said Clementine. 'That's like a holiday.'

'In the library,' Sophie added, as her mother closed the passenger door.

'*Au revoir*,' Odette called.

'Goodbye,' the children chorused as the little van sped off down the driveway.

Lady Clarissa would gladly have kept Sophie and Jules for a week. Jules was a wonderful big brother to Sophie, and he and Clementine got along famously too.

'Come on then, what would you all like for afternoon tea?' Clarissa asked. 'Your father has left me half the patisserie, I think.'

'Chocolate brownie for me,' Sophie said.

'Chocolate eclair for me,' Jules said.

'Is there a meringue?' Clementine was imagining the sweet tingly confection melt away in her mouth.

'Several, I think,' Clarissa nodded.

'Yum! We need to have lots of energy if we're going camping in the library,' said Clementine.

'Why?' Sophie asked, her brown eyes wide.

'Because we're going on a safari,' said Clementine, as if it was obvious. 'Just like Grandpa did when he was young, except we're not going to shoot the animals, we'll just take some photographs.'

Jules laughed. 'So this is another adventure of yours, Clementine. Like last time when you said that all the people in the portraits on the walls had come to life and you told us about them.' Sophie and Jules loved Clementine's stories.

Clementine nodded. The three children followed Lady Clarissa into the entrance hall and Lavender trotted along behind.

'Do you remember when I told you about that lady up there?' Clementine pointed at Aunt Violet's portrait. 'I said that her name was Grace and she was beautiful and kind.'

Sophie and Jules nodded.

'Well, that's not her name.'

Lady Clarissa disappeared into the hallway on her way to the kitchen.

'What is her name?' Sophie asked.

'It's Violet and she's not beautiful. She's snappy and cross, and she's asleep upstairs,' Clementine said.

Sophie and Jules gasped.

'But I thought she was dead, like your grandfather,' Sophie said, her mouth gaping.

'I thought so too, but she came on Friday,' Clementine explained. 'And I don't think she likes me very much and she definitely doesn't like Lavender. She has a sphynx that looks like a giant rat and this afternoon she said that she might like to have my bedroom. But she does wear nice clothes and she has some of the loveliest shoes I've ever seen and she didn't tell on me last night about Mr Sparks's hair.'

'What happened to Mr Sparks's hair?' Sophie asked.

'It's complicated,' Clementine replied. 'I'll tell you later.'

'Maybe she just doesn't know you very well yet,' Jules suggested.

'Maybe, but she really doesn't like Uncle Digby,' Clementine confirmed.

'We should stay out of her way, then,' Jules decided. 'Your house is so big we shouldn't have to see her at all.'

The two girls nodded.

'Come on, let's get something to eat and then we can start building our tents.' Clementine raced off towards the kitchen with Sophie, Jules and Lavender hot on her heels.

CAMPING
OUT

The children had a wonderful afternoon setting up camp in the library. Lavender played hide and seek, running in and out from under the bedsheets that the girls were using to make their tents. Clementine convinced Uncle Digby to light a fire in the library hearth. She told him that a camp wasn't 'proper' unless there was a camp fire and, besides, a chill breath of wind was swirling through the house, a sign of a storm to come. Late in the afternoon, Mrs Mogg appeared

with a delivery of groceries for Lady Clarissa including a giant packet of marshmallows and some extra-long skewers.

By half past five, when Lady Clarissa brought their tea, Clementine, Sophie and Jules had transformed a corner of the enormous library using sheets, pegs and various bits of furniture. Clementine and Sophie had set up their beds under the desk, with a sheet over the top. Jules had a much more elaborate tent. It hung from the gallery upstairs and draped over a padded bench seat, giving him enough space inside to lie down or stand up.

'Well hello, my adventurers,' Lady Clarissa called as she carried in a tray with three plates of creamy scrambled eggs on hot buttered toast. Digby Pertwhistle followed close behind with three steaming mugs of hot chocolate and a bowl of vegetables for Lavender.

'Hello Mummy, hello Uncle Digby.' Clementine poked her head out from under the desk and greeted the pair. 'Do you like our camp site? We're on safari in Africa.'

'Yes, darling, it's wonderful,' Lady Clarissa said, smiling as she surveyed Clementine's stuffed toys, which the children had positioned around the room. 'Look at all those animals! And I love the way you've made your tent two-storeys, Jules. That's terribly clever.'

'I love camping at your house,' Jules replied. 'It's much better than when Papa took us to Gertrude's Grove for a weekend and it rained and rained and our tent had a hole in the roof. At least in here, we won't get wet.'

'Don't bet on it, young man.' Digby Pertwhistle set his tray on a small table beside the desk. 'I heard the forecast was for storms tonight and I was about to get some buckets. Depending on how bad it gets, you might have a drip or two right above your head.'

'Just a couple of drips are okay. On our camping trip we were soaked and Mama said that it was the most terrible weekend of her life,' said Jules as he straightened the sheet.

'All right, big game hunters, come and have your supper while it's hot,' Clarissa called.

'We're not hunters, Mummy,' Clementine said. 'We're wildlife photographers. See?' She reached under the desk and passed her mother an old Polaroid camera.

'Heavens, where did you find that?' Clarissa took it from her daughter and examined the contraption, before giving it back.

'Uncle Digby found it and it still works,' said Clementine. She pointed the camera at her mother, snapped the shutter and a photograph whirred out of the front of the machine.

'Gosh, I think I won that when I was a teenager. I haven't seen it for years but at the time I thought it was the fanciest thing going.' Clarissa laughed at the memory. 'Well, I hope you find some elephants and tigers and maybe even a lion or two in here tonight. But save your shots for the most exciting things because I think the film runs out quite quickly.'

Jules clasped the front of his tent together with two clothes pegs and joined the girls near the fire.

'Would you like Uncle Digby to come back

and tell you a story later?' said Clarissa with a wink at the old man. 'When I was a little girl he used to tell me wonderful tales about African safaris.'

Digby Pertwhistle shook his head. 'Oh, my dear, I think I've almost forgotten about my African adventures.'

'No!' Clementine Rose complained. 'Please tell us a story, Uncle Digby.'

'Yes, please, Uncle Digby,' Sophie added.

Lavender looked up and grunted.

'See, everyone wants you to,' Jules insisted.

'Well, eat your supper and I'll be back with the marshmallows in a little while,' Digby agreed.

Clarissa and Digby retreated to the kitchen and left the children to eat their fireside feast.

A branch outside banged against the window as the wind picked up speed.

'I hate storms,' said Sophie.

'I love them,' Clementine said, as she loaded her fork with a mouthful of scrambled eggs.

'You have to be brave, Sophie,' her brother

told her. 'Like Clementine. The storm can't hurt you.'

'But I don't like the lightning and the thunder,' his sister said. 'It sounds like a giant in a bad temper.'

'I think it's a giant having a party,' Clementine replied. 'Anyway, tonight we're together so nothing can hurt us.'

Jules raised his mug of hot chocolate in the air. 'Let's have a toast to our camping safari.'

Clementine raised her mug and nudged Sophie to do the same.

'To our camping safari,' the girls chorused. Lavender snorted happily.

GHOST SAFARI

At half past eight, after a wonderful tale about mischief-making monkeys and a hippo who liked to eat liquorice, the children brushed their teeth and crawled into their makeshift beds. Outside, the rain had begun to splatter against the windows but within minutes the only noise inside the tents was the shallow breathing of little bodies and a small squeak coming from Lavender, who was also fast asleep.

Clarissa peeked in on the group, switched

off the children's torches and closed the library door.

Aunt Violet had stayed in her room for the rest of the day. Clarissa had taken her a tea tray of boiled eggs and toasty soldiers for her supper, but Violet was fast asleep. Beside her, Pharaoh opened one eye and stared at his hostess, then curled his lip. Clarissa thought Clementine was quite right when she said that he was the strangest creature she'd ever seen.

Clarissa looked at the bags and clothes covering the room. Her aunt certainly had a lot of luggage with her. She walked over to straighten the cushions on the chaise longue and noticed a letter on the desk.

Clarissa leaned in to take a closer look, scanning the page. She glanced towards the bed where her aunt slept. 'So that's why you're here,' she whispered. She couldn't imagine what it would be like to have nowhere to go. And while Aunt Violet was a lot of things, cranky and rude being top of the list, she was also family.

Just after 10 pm, Digby Pertwhistle retired to his room. It wasn't long afterwards that Lady Clarissa made a final check on the children and went up to bed too.

Outside, the wind was beginning to howl. A loose shutter on the far end of the house had started to bang and Clarissa hoped that it didn't wake anyone. She hated the thought of having to go and attend to it in her nightdress, but it wouldn't be the first time. Overhead, thunder rumbled but down in the library the children slept without stirring.

Clementine was in the middle of a lovely dream about her grandpa. She was telling him a new poem she had learned when suddenly lightning tore open the darkness and filled the library with light. She awoke with a start and felt as if she was falling through a giant hole in the sky.

It took her a few moments to remember where she was.

Clementine lay awake under the desk as the light flickered around her. Goosebumps suddenly sprang up along her arms. It wasn't just the storm – she had a feeling there was someone else in the room. She crept to the edge of the tent and pulled open the sheets. A figure dressed in white stood at the end of the room. It had silver hair and bare feet and there was a glow coming from the end of its arm. Clementine wondered if it was one of her ancestors, perhaps from the portraits on the walls. She watched as the ghost pulled some books from the shelf. Clementine rubbed her eyes and wondered if she was still dreaming.

'I knew it,' a voice whispered. 'I knew you were in here. And now you're mine.'

It was the ghost speaking. Clementine reached for the camera beside her.

Sophie stirred. 'What are you doing?' she yawned.

'Shhhh!' Clementine pressed her finger against Sophie's lips. 'There's a ghost out there.'

Sophie's eyes widened. 'A ghost? On our safari?'

'I'm going to take its picture,' Clementine whispered.

Sophie shook her head. 'No!'

'Stay here.' Clementine began to crawl out from under the desk.

The ghost had its back to her. It turned around and at the same time a huge streak of lightning lit up the window and the whole library.

'Oh!' The ghost caught its breath. 'Who's there?' it whispered urgently when it saw Jules's two-storey tent.

Clementine crept in front of the white figure and pressed the button on the camera. The flash went off and Aunt Violet stood frozen to the spot.

'You again! What are you doing?' she demanded.

'Phew!' Clementine let out the breath she had been holding. 'I thought you were a ghost, Aunt Violet!'

Sophie scrambled out from under the desk. 'What's that?' she asked, pointing at Aunt Violet's hand.

Jules was awake now too. He wriggled out of his tent to join the girls. The children had Violet surrounded.

'Go back to sleep,' she ordered. 'You're all dreaming. I am a ghost. You are asleep and I was never here. Now give me that.' She reached out and tried to snatch the photograph that had whirred out of the old camera.

'What's going on in here?' Lady Clarissa flicked on the library lights. 'Aunt Violet! What on earth?'

Digby Pertwhistle hadn't been able to sleep either and was on his way to the kitchen to make a cup of cocoa when he heard the kerfuffle.

'Is that you, Violet?' he asked, squinting at the old woman in her nightgown.

Violet tried to hide whatever it was she was holding behind her back.

But Clementine handed her mother the picture that was coming to life in front of them.

'Is that . . .' Clarissa hesitated, peering at the image. 'Is that the Appleby tiara?' She handed the photograph to Digby Pertwhistle.

'Oh, my dear, I think it is. That tiara and the matching necklace and earrings have been missing for years. Your mother always thought the set had been stolen. You know it's worth a fortune.'

'Is that the tiara Granny's wearing in the portrait?' Clementine asked her mother. 'The one with all the sparkles?' She turned to her great-aunt. 'This morning when you were coming out of my room, Aunt Violet, I saw something twinkly in your hand and then you put it in your pocket. What was that?'

'It was none of your business,' the old woman replied.

'Aunt Violet, please don't speak to Clementine like that. What else did you find?'

'Mummy's earrings,' Violet said, pouting.

'We'll deal with those later. May I have the tiara, please?' Clarissa asked.

'No! It's mine!' the woman snapped.

Digby frowned at her and shook his head softly. 'I think you'll find it belongs to Clarissa.'

'Everything belongs to Clarissa,' Violet yelled. 'The house, the furniture, the china. But this is mine. And so are the earrings and the necklace. I found them when I was little and I hid them in different places in the house. I forgot about them until I was packing up the flat and found an old photograph of Mother wearing them. I couldn't think where the tiara was and then yesterday when I saw that the cabinet was gone, I remembered. You're not having it. I, I, I need it.' Violet's lip trembled and it looked as if she was going to cry.

'Aunt Violet, why don't you give it to me and I'll put it somewhere safe and we can talk about it in the morning,' Clarissa said soothingly.

'No!' The woman shuddered. 'You don't know what it's like. I haven't got any money left. None at all.' Violet began to wail. 'I don't even have anywhere to live!'

'I know,' Clarissa said, as she and Digby exchanged glances.

'It's all right, Aunt Violet,' said Clementine. 'We don't have any money either. And we have plenty of space. You could stay here with us if you like. But you can't have my bedroom,' she added. 'Grandpa said so. And you should try to be a bit kinder, like Mummy said you used to be.'

Violet was cornered. She jammed the tiara on top of Clementine's head and stomped past Clarissa.

'But I'm keeping the earrings, and the necklace too if I can remember where it is,' she said as she turned and stared at the group. Then she fled upstairs to her room.

'Why is Aunt Violet so mad?' Clementine asked her mother.

'I think she's embarrassed,' said Clarissa thoughtfully. 'She's been very sneaky.'

Clementine lifted the tiara from her head and stared at the sparkling jewels. 'It's lovely, Mummy.'

'Yes it is, Clemmie,' her mother replied. 'And I'm going to put it away in a very safe place.'

She strode to the opposite end of the bookshelf, reached up, and rested her hand on the spine of one of the books. The shelf spun around, revealing a safe buried in the wall.

'I think that's a very good idea,' said Digby.

'It's okay, Lady Clarissa, we're on safari,' Jules declared. 'Nothing can get past the wild-life photographers.'

Lady Clarissa spun the dial and swivelled the books back into place. 'All right, off to sleep everyone,' she instructed, 'or you'll never get up in the morning.'

Clementine kissed her mother goodnight and climbed back under the desk. Sophie followed her and Jules disappeared into his tent.

'Would you like to join me for some cocoa, dear?' Digby asked.

'That would be lovely, thank you,' Clarissa replied wearily.

SPECIAL DELIVERY

The next morning the storm had blown away and the sky was a dazzling shade of blue. Clementine, Sophie and Jules slept in until Lavender told them it was time to get up. She made the rounds, pressing her little snout onto the sides of their faces until they stirred.

In the kitchen, Digby Pertwhistle was making tea.

'Hello Uncle Digby,' said Clementine, yawning, as the trio arrived to have breakfast. 'Where's Mummy?'

'She's upstairs talking to Aunt Violet,' the old man said. 'Did you enjoy your safari?'

'It was exciting,' said Clementine, beaming. 'We saw some strange creatures.'

Jules placed three photographs down on the table. He spread them out. Digby laughed.

'Just as well that pig of yours is patient,' he said, marvelling at the pictures. There was Lavender with elephant ears, Lavender with a monkey mask and Lavender wearing a tutu.

'That's a rather unusual animal to find on an African safari,' said Digby, pointing at the one of Lavender in the tutu.

'I thought the tutu might have made her look like a lion but I think she just looks like a ballerina pig,' Clementine sighed.

The doorbell rang.

'I'll get it,' Clemmie yelled and raced out of the kitchen. She almost ran into Aunt Violet and her mother as they reached the bottom of the stairs.

'Good heavens, young lady, you might have killed us,' said Violet, a scowl creasing her face.

'I'm sorry, Aunt Violet. You look nice today,' Clementine said, noticing her great-aunt's white pants-suit and stylish pink shoes.

'Yes, well, I can't say the same for you at the moment.' The old woman shook her head.

Clarissa opened the front door and Clementine skipped across the giant entrance hall to see who was there. A man in a uniform handed her mother an envelope.

'Special delivery for Lady Clarissa Appleby from Cunard's,' the young man announced. 'Please sign here.'

Clarissa scribbled her signature and thanked the fellow, then closed the door.

'What is it, Mummy?' Clementine asked.

'I don't know, but I think we should open it together in the kitchen,' Clarissa smiled.

Violet was standing at the bottom of the stairs looking up at the portraits on the wall.

Clementine stopped and followed her gaze. 'You were lovely.'

'Yes, I was, wasn't I?' The old woman's eyes took on a sparkly sheen.

'Do you want to have some breakfast?' Clementine held out her hand to Aunt Violet.

'Oh, for heaven's sake, I'm perfectly capable of finding my own way to the kitchen – which is where I *presume* we'll be eating, seeing that the dining room is reserved for paying guests,' Violet snapped.

Clementine's lip began to tremble. The old woman caught sight of her and sighed.

'Oh, all right. Come along, Clementine, if it makes you feel better, you can show me the way.'

The old woman reached down and slipped her hand into Clemmie's. There was a spark of electricity between them. 'Oh!' they both gasped in unison. Clemmie giggled and looked up at her great-aunt. She stared at her face, past the wrinkles and the frown lines.

'You know, Aunt Violet, it's funny but we have exactly the same colour eyes, you and me.'

Violet gazed at the child. Her brow furrowed and just for a moment she remembered herself as a young girl and thought she could have been looking into a mirror.

'Well, of course, I am your grandfather's sister, Clementine,' Violet replied. The old woman looked up and caught her niece's gaze. 'Isn't that right, Clarissa?' she said.

Clarissa nodded. 'Of course, Aunt Violet. Now,' she said, changing the subject, 'come along, breakfast's ready.'

'After breakfast you'll have to find Pharaoh for me. He got out last night and he could be anywhere,' Violet informed them.

Clementine gulped. She didn't like the thought of the sphynx lurking about the house.

As Clementine and Aunt Violet followed Clarissa into the kitchen they found Digby, Sophie and Jules huddled together by the back door.

'What *is* it?' Sophie asked, in a confused voice.

'I think it must be that giant rat Clementine was talking about,' Jules whispered.

'Did you say rat?' Aunt Violet strode towards the group. 'That's not a rat, that's my baby.' She stared into the basket and her eyes grew as round as dinner plates. 'Oh, Pharaoh! How could you?' Violet clasped her hand to her mouth.

Clementine ran to see.

'Lavender!' she giggled. 'That's lovely!'

There in the basket, Pharaoh and Lavender were fast asleep. Pharaoh had his paw resting on Lavender's tummy and he was purring like a diesel engine.

'Maybe Pharaoh thinks he's a pig,' Jules said. 'They kind of look the same – except Lavender's much prettier.'

'Wash your mouth out, young man,' Violet rebuked.

'Come and sit down, Aunt Violet, and I'll pour you a cup of tea,' said Clarissa, rolling her eyes at her aunt's theatrics.

'Toast's up,' Digby Pertwhistle called. The children raced back to the kitchen table.

'What did the man deliver?' Clementine

asked her mother, pointing at the envelope that was sitting on the table.

'Oh, I'd almost forgotten about that.' Her mother sat down and picked it up. She ran her finger under the flap and pulled out a letter, which she read aloud. *'Dear Lady Appleby, it is my pleasure to inform you that you are the winner of the Cunard's Coast to Coast Competition.'* Clarissa scanned ahead silently.

'But what did you win, Mummy?' said Clementine, fizzing with excitement.

Sophie looked on beside her friend, and Jules raced over to stand behind Clarissa and read over her shoulder.

'Goodness! It's a cruise. On board the Queen Mary 2, all the way around the world. It's for three whole months!' Clarissa exclaimed. 'I can't go, of course. What about you, Digby?'

The old man pursed his lips and shook his head. 'Couldn't possibly leave you and the little one for that long.'

'I would get seasick,' Jules piped up.

Aunt Violet was on the edge of her seat. 'The Queen Mary 2, you say? When I was a young woman I sailed on the original Queen Mary,' she said. 'With your father and our parents, actually. It was one of the happiest times we ever had as a family.'

Clementine skipped around to the end of the table and pulled on her mother's arm. She whispered something in her ear.

Clarissa gave her daughter a broad smile. 'Yes, I think that's a lovely idea, Clemmie.'

'Aunt Violet,' said Clementine happily, 'would you like to go on a long holiday?'

Violet frowned and looked from Clementine to her niece. 'Really? You'd do that for me, Clarissa?'

Clarissa nodded and handed Clementine the letter, which she took around to her great-aunt.

'That's . . . that's very kind.' Aunt Violet wiped her hand across the corner of her eye.

Clementine smiled at her mother and then at Uncle Digby. He gave her a knowing wink.

'But you can wipe those silly smiles off your faces. Three months is not forever, you know.' Violet sniffed and straightened her shoulders. 'Just you wait and see. I'll be back.'

CAST OF CHARACTERS

The Appleby household

Clementine Rose
   Appleby

Five-year-old
   daughter of
   Lady Clarissa

Lavender

Clemmie's teacup pig

Lady Clarissa Appleby

Clementine's mother
   and owner of
   Penberthy House

Digby Pertwhistle

Butler at Penberthy
   House

| Aunt Violet Appleby | Clementine's grandfather's sister |
| Pharaoh | Aunt Violet's beloved sphynx |

Friends and village folk

Margaret Mogg	Owner of the Penberthy Floss village shop
Clyde Mogg	Margaret's husband
Claws Mogg	Margaret's tabby cat
Father Bob	Village minister
Adrian	Father Bob's dribbly bulldog
Pierre Rousseau	Owner of Pierre's Patisserie in Highton Mill
Odette Rousseau	Wife of Pierre and mother of Jules and Sophie
Jules Rousseau	Seven-year-old brother of Sophie

Sophie Rousseau	Clementine's best friend – also five years old
Mintie	Sophie's white kitten
Poppy Bauer	Clementine's friend who lives on the farm at Highton Hall

Hotel guests

Mr and Mrs Floyd and Zelda Sparks

Miss Becca Herring

Mr and Mrs Edward and Sandra O'Connell

ABOUT THE AUTHOR

Jacqueline Harvey taught for many years in girls' boarding schools. She is the author of the bestselling Alice-Miranda series and the Clementine Rose series, and was awarded Honour Book in the 2006 Australian CBC Awards for her picture book *The Sound of the Sea*. She now writes full-time and is working on more Alice-Miranda and Clementine Rose adventures.

www.jacquelineharvey.com.au

Collect the series

Loved the book?

There's so much more
stuff to check out online